To Carol Southern, with love and gratitude always   KH *and* HC
Also love and thanks to Paul Craig for valuable advice   HC

Published by Pleasant Company Publications
© 2001 HIT Entertainment PLC
Text copyright © 1989 Katharine Holabird
Illustrations copyright © 1989 Helen Craig

Visit our Web site at **www.americangirl.com**
and Angelina's very own site at **www.angelinaballerina.com**

Second Edition
Printed in Italy.
02 03 04 05 06 07 08 09 LEGO 12 11 10 9 8 7 6 5

Library of Congress Cataloging-in-Publication Data
Craig, Helen.
[Angelina's birthday surprise]
Angelina's birthday / illustrations by Helen Craig ;
story by Katharine Holabird.
p. cm.
Summary: Angelina the dancing mouse discovers what a special day a birthday can be.
ISBN 1-58485-652-1
[1. Mice—Fiction. 2. Birthdays—Fiction.]
I. Holabird, Katharine. II. Title.
PZ7.C84418 Aq 2001
[E]—dc21   00-044106

Angelina's Birthday

Story by **Katharine Holabird** Illustrations by **Helen Craig**

PLEASANT
COMPANY
PUBLICATIONS™

Angelina loved her bicycle and rode it everywhere. The bicycle had belonged to Aunt Amy and it was quite old, but Angelina thought it was the best bicycle in the world.

One morning, she pedaled as fast as she could over to Alice's house.

"Next week will be my birthday, and we're going to have a picnic!" Angelina announced to Alice. "My mother said we could go to the village today and buy decorations."

Alice jumped on her bicycle, and they rode quickly down the road to Mrs. Thimble's General Store.

"Another birthday, Angelina!" Mrs. Thimble chuckled as she showed the girls the party decorations. "My, but you're getting old!" Angelina smiled as she paid for the streamers and balloons. She really did feel a lot older now that she could ride her bike so well and was sent on important errands to the village.

"Come on, Angelina, let's have a race!" called Alice.

Angelina loved to race Alice down the bumpy road home. "I'll beat you, Alice!" Angelina shouted, going so fast that she didn't see the big rock lying directly in her path.

BANG!

The bike crashed into the rock. Angelina flew into the air and then fell to the ground with a terrible bump.

"OOOOOOOOH! Why did you make me race, Alice!" cried Angelina angrily, pointing to a cut on her foot.

Poor Alice was very upset. She took Angelina's hand and helped her stand up. They looked at the bicycle. One wheel had come off, the other was twisted, and the handlebars were upside down.

"Maybe we can fix it," said Alice.

They dragged the broken bicycle back to Angelina's house, where Mr. Mouseling bandaged Angelina's foot and shook his head. "That must have been quite a crash," he said.

"What shall I do?" Angelina asked sadly.

Mrs. Mouseling smiled at her. "Perhaps you're old enough now to help earn some money to buy a new bicycle."

"I'll try," Angelina agreed, and she made a list of all the jobs she could do. Alice offered to help.

On Monday after school, Angelina planted strawberries and raspberries for Mrs. Hodgepodge.

On Tuesday afternoon, Angelina helped her ballet teacher, Miss Lilly, wash the dance floor and polish the piano.

On Wednesday, Angelina and Alice watered the garden and hung out the washing for Alice's mother, who had a new baby.

On Thursday, they mowed the grass and picked apples for Angelina's grandparents.

On Friday, Angelina and Alice helped Mr. Bell, the old postman, repair and paint his front door. Then they walked to Mrs. Thimble's store for more balloons.

Angelina was happy. She felt so proud of their hard work and the money they had earned. Then they passed the bicycle shop. There in the window was the most beautiful bicycle Angelina had ever seen. But it was very expensive. Angelina counted all her money. "I haven't even got enough to buy a nice horn for that bike."

"I wish I could buy the bicycle for you," said Alice.

Saturday afternoon was Angelina's birthday party.
Alice came early to help blow up the balloons
and decorate the garden. Angelina's mother and
Aunt Amy had made a delicious picnic, and soon
Angelina's friends started arriving.

Flora and Felicity brought Angelina hair ribbons
and a book on dancing. Alice gave her a delicate
ballerina doll. Cousin Henry gave Angelina a
silver horn for when she got another bicycle.
Angelina managed to smile and hug Henry,
because she knew that he was trying to be kind.

The party games began. The garden filled with singing voices,

"HAPPY BIRTHDAY, ANGELINA!
HAPPY BIRTHDAY TO YOU . . ."

Angelina saw her grandparents, followed by Mrs. Hodgepodge, Miss Lilly,
Mrs. Thimble, Alice's mother, Mr. Bell, and Aunt Amy, all with bicycles!
"We came to have a race with you, Angelina," said her grandmother.

Angelina was surprised. "I'd love to go," she said,
"but I don't have a new bike yet." She felt like crying.

"Angelina! Come and look!" shouted Henry,
who had a terrible time keeping secrets.

And there, hidden behind the garden shed, was the
shiny new bicycle that Angelina and Alice had seen
in the bicycle shop window.

"Oh!" Angelina was so excited she jumped on the bicycle and rode it in circles around and around the garden.

Her grandfather smiled at her and said, "You and Alice worked so hard we all wanted to help buy the bicycle for your birthday."

Then Angelina led everyone on a birthday bicycle
ride over the hills, singing all the way, with
balloons and streamers flying in the wind.